The BIG Red Squirrel

and the

Little Rhinoceros

for Bodula

The Big Red Squirrel and the Little Rhinoceros

By Mischa Damjan

Illustrated by Ralph Steadman

First published in Great Britain in 1965

This edition published in 2009 by
Pavilion Children's Books
10 Southcombe Street
London
W14 0RA

An imprint of Anova Books Company Ltd

ISBN: 978-1-84365-130-7

A CIP catalogue record for this book is available from the British Library.

10 9 8 7 6 5 4 3 2 1

Printed and bound by SNP Leefung Printers Ltd, China
Colour Reproduction by Dot Gradations Ltd, UK

This book can be ordered direct from the publisher at the website: www.anovabooks.com,
or try your local bookshop.

The **BIG** Red Squirrel and the Little Rhinoceros

Mischa Damjan

Illustrated by
Ralph STEADman

PAVILION
CHILDREN'S

As the sun was rising from behind the hill, red and round like a balloon over the Forest of the Thousand Shadows, the Rhinoceros felt an itch on the back of his head.

This is where our story begins...

Enraged by the tiresome itch, the Rhinoceros charged against a tree. High up amid the topmost branches of that very tree, a little Red Squirrel was peacefully sleeping.

Thump,

thump,

thump...

The earth was quaking.

Crash!

The tree was torn up by its roots,
and the little Red Squirrel sent
sprawling on the hard ground.
"Oh, no!" wailed the Red Squirrel.
"Not that noisy Rhinoceros again!"
But the Rhinoceros only laughed at him.

At the same time, the Mouse woke up with a start.
"It's that tyrant again," he sighed, crawling out of his hole.

Outside, there was the Lion roaring like a hurricane:

"I am Leo the Great,

I am Leo the Mighty,

I am Leo, Ruler of all!"

The Mouse crouched even lower and squeaked: "Brother, you frighten me!"

But the Lion ignored him and kept on roaring until the whole jungle shivered.

Roar!

At last the Lion noticed the Mouse and, stretching full length in the sand, asked mockingly: "What can I do for you my giant friend?"

"You know, Leo, you gave me and my family such a fright!" said the Mouse sadly. The Lion laughed gleefully. "Leo, the strong ought to help the weak, that's the only way of proving their strength," continued the Mouse, even sadder than before.

The Lion laughed even more gleefully and
lashed out at the ground with his shaggy tail so
that the earth shook and the sand flew to left and right.

For a while the Mouse stood silently. Then he turned
about and ran away.

In the same forest and on the same day the Frog sat on his leaf and trembled with fear. For, not far away, the Crocodile sat and chattered his teeth terribly.

"There's no peace with you chattering your teeth. Please, do stop it!" stammered the Frog.

The Crocodile laughed gleefully and chattered even louder.

"I'm so frightened that I find no pleasure in singing in the evening!" croaked the Frog.

At that the Crocodile laughed even more gleefully and chattered his teeth even more terribly.

When the stars were tidily hung in the sky, the Red Squirrel and the Mouse and the Frog set out to collect all the small animals for a meeting.

Soon they all stood together in the dark night: the Red Squirrel and the Mouse, the Cuckoo and the Worm, the Hedgehog and the Frog, the Snail and the Grasshopper, with the Wren sitting on a flower.

The Red Squirrel spoke first: "I want to be big, to defy the Rhinoceros. I want to get even with him!"

Then the Frog spoke: "I want to be big to get even with the Crocodile!"

And the Cuckoo added: "I want to be big so that I can leave my eggs without fear in whatever nest I like!"

At last
the Wren
twittered:
"I want to be big,
just for a change!"

And now the unbelievable happened…

As the sun was again rising from behind the hill, red and round like a balloon, everything was different in the Forest of the Thousand Shadows.

The

BIG

Rhinoceros

had

become

tiny,

while the little Red Squirrel had grown to a great height.

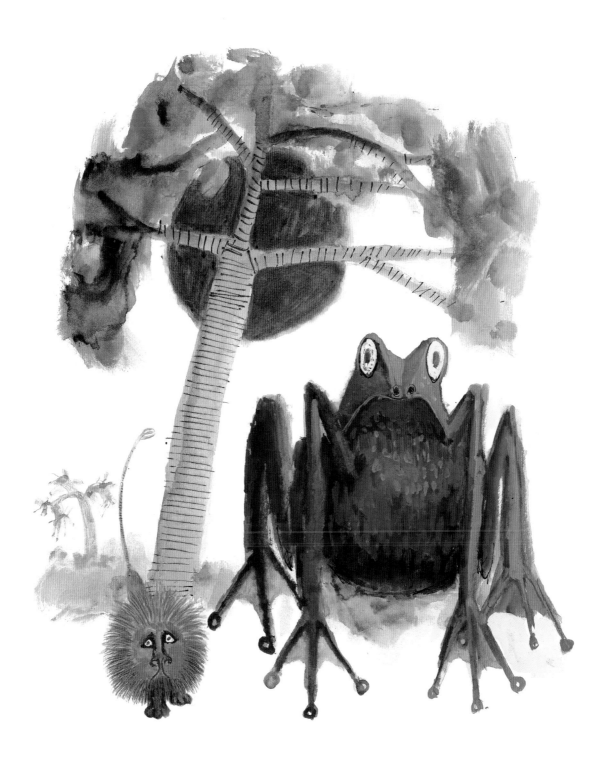

At the same time the Lion and the Crocodile became very small
while the Frog and the Mouse became...

HUGE!

Almost at once, the
Red Squirrel was in difficulty
because the smaller branches would break
under his weight. Life in the trees was
becoming a nightmare for him. What's more, the
poor Red Squirrel had to work ceaselessly to feed
himself and his ever-hungry giant children. Far from
dreaming of vengeance against the Rhinoceros, the
Red Squirrel now dreamt of the good old times when
he had been in the habit of leaping from one branch to
another with no effort at all, gathering nuts or looking
down at the big animals, while boldly sitting in the tops
of the highest trees.

That's what it had been like. But now the Red Squirrel
was sadly squatting on the ground, deeply ashamed of
his wish for revenge. The little Rhinoceros was very
unhappy, too. In the old days, everybody had been
afraid of him, but now he himself was living in
constant fear. Even the croaking of the giant
Frog made him tremble. The little
Rhinoceros fled into a hole, bitterly
regretting his bad behaviour.

Then the day came when the little Rhinoceros again felt an itch on the back of his head, and charged wrathfully against a big tree. Instead of uprooting it, however, he fell headlong in the dust.

And what about the giant Mouse? He was standing in front of his house, unable to get in – the hole had become too small. He had no choice but to build a new house, which was not an easy task at all: there was a lot of work to do and the earth was heavy to move.

So now the Mouse toiled day and night, feeling very unhappy about his wish to be bigger.

Suddenly, the Lion felt hungry, but he couldn't hunt. "Do I have to eat grass like a donkey?" he grumbled. This annoyed the former King so much that he lashed out at the ground with his little tail. But the earth did not shake. Not even a single blade of grass moved.

The Cuckoo, too, was unhappy about his wish to be big, as things were becoming difficult for his wife. She could no longer lay her eggs in other birds' nests, because now her eggs were far too big! It was a real disaster!

And the big Frog sat in his small pool and bitterly complained about his life. He had grown so big and the flies were so small that he had to hunt all day long and he was still hungry.

Even the giant Wren was not content. Since he was clumsy and heavy he no longer heard people say: "You sweet little bird!" And this made him unhappy.

So the animals in the Forest of the Thousand Shadows were all unhappy. Something had to be done. They all gathered together and longed for the old days.

And then it happened…

When the sun rose again from behind the hill, red and round like a balloon, things had changed in the Forest of the Thousand Shadows: the big animals were big again, and the little animals were little.

And the Lion happened to come across the Mouse.

"Good morning, my friend," said the Lion, "What can I do for you?"

"How kind of you to ask," squeaked the Mouse, smiling.

And that same morning the Rhinoceros
again felt an itch on the back of his head.
Slowly and carefully he approached the tree
occupied by the Red Squirrel, looked up and said,
"Please may I rub against your tree?"
"Please do," said the Red Squirrel.
The Rhinoceros smiled and gently scratched
his head on the tree.

And from that day on in the Forest of the
Thousands Shadows the big animals and
the small animals had learned to live
together happily.